W9-AZG-228

Dear Reader,

I hope you are enjoying the Little Rhino series!

This story means a lot to me because I'll never forget my first baseball bat. It was a black bat, and I took care of it like it was the most important thing in the world to me. I would talk to my bat, clean my bat . . . I would even sleep with my bat! When I held that bat, it felt like it was made just for me. I loved that it was going to help me hit home runs far out of the park.

My bat was my responsibility. When you are part of a team, you have to learn how to be responsible. It is important to show up to practice and games on time with all of your equipment. That is as much a part of being a good teammate as encouraging the people you play with to be successful and to have fun. When you're having fun, that's when you start winning games.

Ryan Howard

Krystle Howard

LITTLE Rhino

by **RYAN HOWARD**
and **KRYSTLE HOWARD**

● **BOOK TWO** ●
THE BEST BAT

SCHOLASTIC PRESS/NEW YORK

To Darian and Ariana. We love you.

— R.H. & K.H.

ISBN 978-0-545-67494-2

12 11 10 9 8 7 6 5 4 3 2 1   15 16 17 18 19 20/0

Printed in the U.S.A.   113
First printing, April 2015
Book design by Christopher Stengel

· CHAPTER 1 ·
A Big Change

*B*ring *it on,* Little Rhino thought.

Baseball season was here! Rhino and his teammates had been practicing for two weeks. Finally, Saturday's game would be for real.

Rhino had hit a game-winning home run in the Mustangs' practice game a few days earlier. He'd also made a great catch in center field. He felt confident. He was ready. Today's practice session was the last one before the opener.

"I'm going to smack another homer," Rhino said. "My new bat is awesome."

The bat was a gift from Grandpa James. He had surprised Rhino with it that morning. "You earned this," Grandpa had said. Rhino had received excellent grades on his latest progress report. He worked just as hard in the classroom as he did on the baseball field. Rhino was so happy. The bat felt perfect when he swung it—almost like it was part of his body. It was the right weight and length for him, and it cut smoothly through the air.

The day was warm and sunny. Rhino pulled off his sweatshirt. He untucked his baggy white T-shirt out from his shorts. The team didn't practice in their uniforms. Then Rhino wrapped his hoodie around the new bat he had with him and set it on the dugout bench. He and his best friend, Cooper, were the first players to arrive at the field, as usual.

"Let's catch, Rhino," Cooper said. "We need to warm up." "Rhino" was the nickname that everyone used, even though his real name was Ryan.

They tossed a ball back and forth. Coach Ray and his daughter, Bella, arrived a minute later. Other players started to trickle in, too. They were all wearing their bright blue caps with the big *M* for Mustangs.

Bella trotted over and winked at Rhino. "Hey, Cooper," she said, flipping her brown ponytail. "Mind if we switch? I need to work with my outfield partner." Bella had played right field in the practice game.

"Sure," Cooper replied. He looked around for someone else to throw with.

Bella punched her glove and said, "Fire it here, Rhino."

After everyone had warmed up, Coach started a drill. "We need to develop quick hands," he said. He had one player in each group send a fast ground ball to the other.

"Field it cleanly, then release it fast," Coach said. "A quick throw can make the difference between an out and a base runner."

They worked on that for several minutes, then Coach sent the starters out to their positions. It was time for batting practice. "Play it like a real game," Coach said. "Run out every hit. You'll all get plenty of chances to swing the bat today."

Rhino sprinted to center field. He was so excited that he hopped up and down, waiting to make his first catch of the day.

He didn't wait long. The first batter looped a soft fly ball over the head of the second baseman. It looked like it would drop for a single, but Rhino darted after it.

The ball hung in the air just long enough for Rhino to get under it. He reached out his glove on the run and made the catch, then tossed the ball back to the pitcher.

"Incredible speed," said Bella, who had run over to back him up. "No one's going to get a hit if you're out here!"

Rhino blushed. *What's up with Bella lately being all nicey nice?* He trotted back to his position.

He caught another fly ball and fielded two grounders that got through for singles. Then Coach waved the three outfielders in to bat.

Rhino grabbed his new bat. He stood with Bella while their teammate named Carlos took his turn at the plate. Carlos was the smallest player on the team, but he was a good fielder.

"Nice bat," Bella said to Rhino. "Brand-new?"

Rhino nodded. "It's the best bat," he said. He handed it to Bella for a look.

"Too heavy," Bella said.

"It's just right for me," Rhino replied.

Rhino studied the pitcher. Dylan was a wise guy and often a bully, but he was a good athlete. He'd given Rhino a hard time early in the season, but lately he minded his own business.

I still don't trust him, but he is my teammate, Rhino's thinker said. Grandpa had taught Rhino to always use his head and think things through.

Dylan took off his cap and wiped the sweat off

his forehead. He smirked at the batter, put his cap back on, and wound up to pitch.

Carlos swung and missed. Dylan laughed. His next pitch was a strike, too. Carlos finally hit a weak ground ball that Dylan fielded. His throw to first was a little high, and it bounced off the first baseman's glove and dropped to the ground.

"Don't be afraid of the ball!" Dylan yelled at the first baseman, Paul.

Paul stared at his glove and ran his other hand through his curly red hair. He had dropped another throw earlier, and he did not seem confident about playing first base.

Bella was up next and struck out. She frowned as she walked past Rhino on his way to the plate. "He's got good stuff today," she said. "Tough to hit." Dylan glared at Rhino. Rhino glared back.

Dylan is always so confident that he'll get the best of everyone, said Rhino's thinker. *I'll show him.*

Rhino stopped beside home plate. He took his bat and pointed to the outfield. "That's where this one is going," he said. Dylan shot him a dirty look as Rhino picked up a helmet from the backstop and walked around the base to get into his batting stance.

The first pitch was high and way inside. Rhino leaned back and let it go by.

The second pitch was low and outside. Rhino shook his head. "Put it in here!" he said.

"Right past you," Dylan said. He wound up and fired the ball.

The pitch was waist-high and straight down the middle. Rhino timed his swing perfectly. With a sharp *crack* the ball soared high over the field. There was no question where it was headed.

Rhino ran toward first base. He was only half-way there as the ball flew over the center field fence. His teammates cheered. Dylan kicked at the pitcher's mound and frowned.

"Good contact!" Coach called. He put up his hands and told Rhino to stop. "No need to run that one out," he said. "Take another swing or two."

Rhino went back to the batter's box. He smirked at Dylan. Dylan scowled even deeper. He slung another pitch toward the plate.

Thwack!

This time Rhino hit it deep into left field, where it crashed against the fence. He raced around first base and slid into second, safely ahead of the throw.

Rhino had hit a homer and a double on two straight pitches! He scored on Cooper's single a few minutes later.

"Should I go back to center field?" he asked.

Coach waved Rhino over. "I'm thinking about making a switch," he said.

"What kind of switch?"

"I'd like you to try another position," Coach said. "It's important for players to try different positions to see where they fit best."

Rhino nodded. He would do anything to help the team. "Left field instead of center?" he asked. Rhino knew that his strong throwing arm might be more valuable in left.

Coach smiled. "A bigger switch than that," he said. "I was thinking about the infield."

Rhino gulped. He'd played third base one day in practice and didn't like it very much.

"I know you are very capable of playing outfield. You're a great fielder," Coach said.

Rhino let out a long breath. "Which position?" he asked.

"First base," Coach said. "That's a key spot, and a natural one for a lefty like you. Having you in there could save us some trouble. Paul will do better at a position that has less pressure."

But can I deal with the pressure? Rhino wondered. There was lots of pressure on a first baseman. Rhino would have to field sharp grounders, handle quick throws from the other infielders, and catch long tosses from the outfielders.

Rhino loved playing center field. "Okay," he said. "I'll try first base."

But I probably won't like it, he thought.

Then his thinker really went to work. *If it's best for the team, then it's best for me. I'll work hard at it and make it pay off.*

CHAPTER 2

Switching Things Up

Rhino felt butterflies as he took his spot near first base. Cooper was still there after hitting his single. He was taller than Rhino and just as fast.

Cooper took a few steps from the base. "Hit it in the outfield and I'll score," he said softly. Cooper was talking to himself, but Rhino heard.

"Here comes a double play," Rhino said with a laugh. "You're out of here."

Paul was at bat. His curly red hair stuck out the sides of the batting helmet. He was a lefty, like Rhino, which was one of the reasons Coach had tried him at first base before he made a couple of errors.

I'll do better playing first base than he did, Rhino thought. *I hope!*

Paul swung hard at the first pitch and caught just a piece of it. It rolled along the first baseline and dribbled foul. Rhino scooped it up. He faked a throw to Dylan, then playfully tagged Cooper. "You're out!" he said.

Cooper laughed. "Play ball," he said. He was standing squarely on the base. He wasn't out at all. Dylan signaled for the ball back. He shook his head at Rhino and Cooper like he didn't want to see anyone else having a good time. Rhino tossed the ball back and got set, a few feet from the base. Cooper took a few steps toward second.

Paul made solid contact this time, and the ball rocketed up the same line. Cooper ran for second. Rhino leaped for the ball, reaching his glove over his head.

Whack! The ball landed firmly in Rhino's glove for an out.

Rhino scrambled to his knees. Cooper was running back toward first. If Rhino could get there ahead of him, he'd force him out.

Their feet seemed to hit the base at the same time. Coach yelled, "Out!" and Rhino raised his glove in triumph. His first play at the new position was an unassisted double play!

"Nice one!" Coach said. "Looks like first base might work pretty well for you."

Rhino felt a surge of confidence. Cooper walked off the field, shaking his head.

There's no stopping me now, Rhino thought. *Hitting, fielding, I can do it all. Major League Baseball here I come.*

But things didn't quite work that way. The next batter hit a grounder to the shortstop. The throw to first base was low and bounced in the dirt. It hit Rhino's glove and rolled away, and the runner was safe.

Shake it off, Rhino's thinker said. *Get the next one.*

A short while later, Dylan had to charge in for a ball that skipped slowly toward the pitcher's mound. The runner was fast, and Dylan's throw to first was off target. Rhino stretched as far as he could, but there was no way he could keep his foot on the base. He lunged for the ball and caught it, but the runner beat him to the base.

"Stay on the bag!" Dylan yelled. "He was safe because of you."

"I'm not made of rubber bands!" Rhino yelled back. "My arm only stretches so far. Make a better throw!"

"Calm down, guys," Coach said. "That was a tough play. Yelling at your teammate doesn't help anything."

Rhino let out his breath in a huff. *Dylan's mad because I always hit home runs when he's pitching. Maybe pointing my new bat into the outfield was too much, but he can't blame me for his terrible throw.*

After practice, Coach gathered the team in the dugout. "I want everyone to be here at least a half

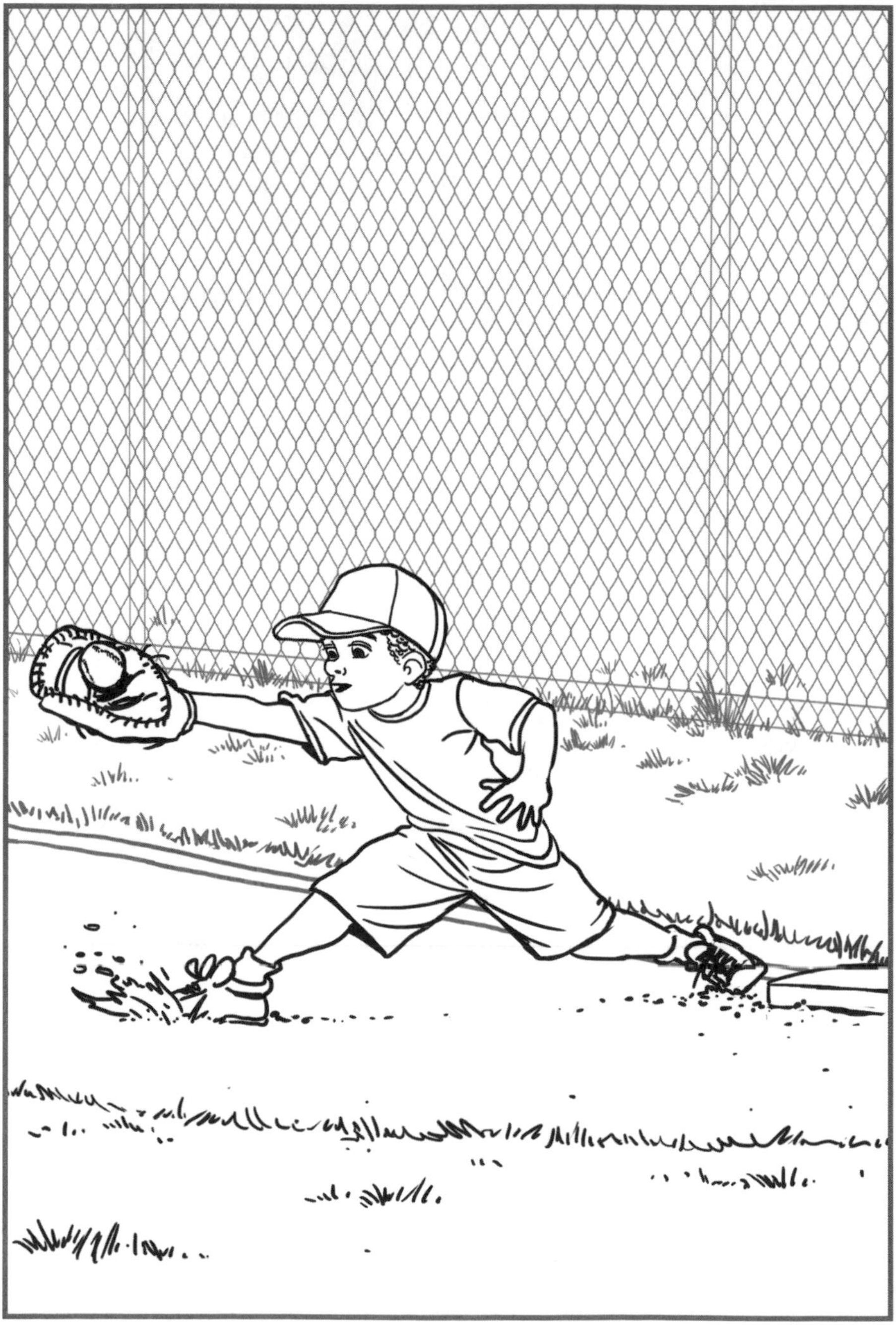

hour before the game on Saturday," he said. "Be suited up from head to toe: baseball socks, cleats, uniform, cap. And remember, this is a *team*. We all support one another."

Rhino knew that last comment was meant for him and Dylan. Rhino wasn't upset about being reminded to act like a good teammate, but Dylan stomped off the field toward the dugout.

As the other players departed, Coach asked Rhino and Cooper to stay for a few minutes.

"I'll show you a few things about playing first base," Coach said. He sent Cooper to shortstop.

"I'll put the equipment away, Dad," Bella said.

Coach showed Rhino where to stand. "You're quick, so you can play somewhat deep," he said. "You can usually outrun anyone to the base."

Coach tossed a ball to Cooper. "Watch me," he said to Rhino.

As Cooper threw the ball, Coach stepped onto first base and held up his glove. "Keep that foot planted," he said to Rhino. "Only leave the base if the throw is off-line."

"Like that throw from Dylan?"

"Right," Coach said. "But on a good throw, always keep your foot on the base."

Rhino took several throws from Cooper. Most of them were on target. The fourth throw was too high, and Rhino jumped. His foot missed the base when he landed, but he found it in a second.

"As you get used to the position, you'll have a natural feel for where the base is," Coach said. "You'll be great at it, but it takes a while to learn."

Rhino grinned. He'd had a good practice, despite a couple of rough spots. Those two big hits had been the highlights.

"The equipment's all packed," Bella said to her father. She handed Rhino a bottle of water. "We had an extra," she said with a smile.

"Thanks," Rhino said. He took a long drink, then waved to Coach and Bella as they drove off.

"Let's go," Cooper said, nudging Rhino. "I'm thirsty and starving. Bella didn't give *me* an extra water bottle."

Rhino walked to the dugout to get his stuff. He picked up his sweatshirt, and his heart sank.

His brand-new bat was missing.

CHAPTER 3

Who's to Blame?

Rhino walked slowly up the driveway at Grandpa James's house. He and Cooper had searched everywhere for the new bat. Under the dugout bench. Behind the dugout. In the dirt outside the field.

Dylan! Rhino was sure Dylan had taken, it. He'd been angry that Rhino had hit that home run and a double. This was Dylan's way of getting back at him.

Now Rhino had to face Grandpa James. He found him in the backyard, raking a large rectangular area of dirt that he'd marked off with stakes.

"Why so glum?" Grandpa asked.

Rhino started to speak but stopped. He looked over at his brother, C.J.

C.J. was twelve. He looked like Rhino but was taller. C.J. had played in the same baseball league that Rhino was in now. Rhino hoped he could be as good of a player as his brother.

"Did you strike out?" asked C.J.

"No," Rhino said. "I hit really well today. But . . ."

"But what?" Grandpa said.

"My bat's gone."

"Did it break?" Grandpa asked.

"No." Rhino looked down at his feet. "After practice, Coach had me stay a few minutes to work on fielding. When we were finished, my bat was missing."

"Did your coach pack it up with the other equipment by mistake?" C.J. asked.

Rhino brightened. "Maybe. Can we check?"

They headed for the house. Rhino glanced back at the yard. It looked like Grandpa was expanding the size of his garden. Rhino hoped there would still be enough room for batting practice and playing catch. Baseball in the yard with Grandpa was one his favorite things.

Grandpa called Coach Ray. He explained what happened, and Coach said he'd call back. But after Coach had taken a look, he called to say that the bat wasn't with the other equipment.

"I know it was Dylan," Rhino said. "He's the only mean one on the team."

Grandpa was still on the phone with Coach Ray. Coach said he'd call Dylan's house and see what he could find out.

But that call didn't help, either. "Dylan promised your coach that he didn't touch the bat," Grandpa said. "Your coach believes him."

"I don't," Rhino said.

"You don't have any evidence," Grandpa said.

"Sure I do!" Rhino replied. "Dylan is always being a pain. Today he yelled at me when *he* made a bad throw. And he was angry because I smacked his pitches like a Major League Baseball player."

Grandpa folded his arms across his chest. "First of all, the bat is your responsibility. Second, it's not fair to accuse someone of being a thief."

"But he is."

Grandpa cleared his throat. "Remember last Halloween? C.J. blamed you for eating all of the peanut butter cups. How did that make you feel?"

Rhino glanced at C.J., who was fighting back a smile. "Not good," Rhino said. "That was different. I didn't eat them."

"But he said you did."

C.J. nodded. "Yeah, and when Grandpa found out I hid the candy to keep it all for myself, I ended up with no peanut butter cups because he took them all back!" he said.

Grandpa nodded. "And you learned your lesson, C.J." Grandpa looked at Rhino. "The bat might turn up. Maybe another player took it home by mistake. In the meantime, you'll go back to using the team's bats."

Rhino knew that whatever had happened to his bat, Grandpa was right about one thing. *My bat, my responsibility,* Rhino's thinker said. He'd do his best to find out what became of the bat, but he'd try not to blame anyone else, especially Dylan.

That bat sure felt great when he swung it, though. He wanted nothing more than to get it back before the Mustang's first real game.

Rhino went up to his room and sat on the bed. He tried to get excited about the game, but he couldn't stop thinking about the bat.

The bedroom door was open. C.J. knocked anyway. He and Rhino looked a lot alike—lean and strong—but C.J. was bigger, of course. "You can use one of my bats," he said. C.J. played shortstop for the middle-school team. He'd outgrown the bat Grandpa had given him when he was Rhino's age.

"Thanks," Rhino said. But he decided to use the team's bats. He wouldn't want to lose one of C.J.'s. "I'll do fine. I hit a homer with one of the team's bats last time. I'm just nervous. It's our first game of the season and this isn't a great way to start off."

"That's true," C.J. said.

C.J. stood in the doorway but didn't say anything more. Rhino could tell that his brother felt bad for him. That helped a little.

"I'll be right back," C.J. said.

When he returned, C.J. was holding something behind his back. He had a big grin.

"What?" Rhino said.

"I was saving these for my dessert," C.J. said. He held out his hand. "For you."

C.J. handed Rhino a package of peanut butter cups.

Rhino laughed. "Are these from Halloween?" he asked.

"Grandpa never gave those back to me. I think *he* ate them all," C.J. said. "I bought these today."

"Thanks," Rhino said. He was starting to feel hungry. "Two in a pack. We'll split them after dinner."

"Right. Grandpa made spaghetti and meatballs. Let's get fueled. I have a game on Saturday, too!"

· CHAPTER 4 ·
Confusing Clues

Rhino checked his cubby at school on Friday and was surprised to find a note in an envelope. He sat at his desk to read it.

Missing something?
Pay attention to the clues!
CLUE 1: Your bat flew away after practice.

I already know that, Rhino thought. Then his thinker worked harder. *After practice Coach had me do some extra work. That's when I wasn't paying attention to the bat.*

But that didn't help to solve anything.

Rhino stared at the note. Who had written it? He turned in his seat to face Cooper.

"We need to get a sample of Dylan's handwriting," Rhino said, showing Cooper the note. "If it matches this, then I'll have proof that he took my bat."

Cooper thought for a few seconds. "That girl Kerry from our dinosaur group is in Dylan's class," he said. "We can ask her to help."

The dinosaur group met in the cafeteria at lunchtime. Rhino and Cooper had joined a few weeks earlier. They loved the lively discussions about stegosaurs and sauropods and giant meat-eaters.

"Great idea," Rhino said. He always looked forward to lunchtime anyway. Now he had an extra reason.

The morning seemed to go very slowly. Rhino couldn't concentrate on the math and science lessons. He'd have to do some extra reading at home. Schoolwork always came first in their house.

At lunchtime, Rhino hurried to the cafeteria. He was starving. Whatever was cooking smelled delicious.

Bella and Kerry were already at the dinosaur table. Bella winked at Rhino, but he was too busy trying to get Kerry's attention to notice. He sat down between the two girls.

"I need a favor," Rhino said to Kerry.

"Sure thing," Kerry said. She had black braids and often led the dinosaur discussions, and she always wore the brightest shirts in the cafeteria. Today's shirt was the same color as a lemon.

"I need a copy of Dylan's handwriting," Rhino said. "Can you get him to write something for you?"

"That's kind of strange. What for?" Kerry asked.

Bella looked at Rhino. "Yeah, Why do you need that? Maybe I can help, too?"

Rhino looked at his two friends. "Someone took my bat from practice."

Bella nodded. "My dad mentioned that."

"Whoever took it left me a note about it," Rhino said. "I think Dylan took it, but I don't have proof. If his handwriting matches the note, then I'll know it was him."

"I'll write out a riddle and pass it to Dylan," Kerry said. "He'll write out the answer, then we'll have what you need."

"You probably just misplaced the bat," Bella said. "I don't think anyone on our team would take it."

"We looked everywhere," Rhino said.

Bella took a bite of her sandwich. She turned to Kerry and said, "What's the topic today? T. rex again?"

"Allosaurus," Kerry replied. "They were smaller than T. rex, but much faster. And mean."

Mean, Rhino thought. *Like Dylan. But with Kerry's help, I'll get to the bottom of this. That note will be all the evidence I need. Dylan thinks he's slick, but I'll show him.*

After lunch, Rhino passed Dylan in the hall-way as he was going back to his classroom. To his surprise, Dylan pointed at him and said, "Go, Mustangs."

Rhino glared at him.

Back in class, Rhino opened his desk to take out his reading book. There was another note. It was in the same writing as the first one.

CLUE 2: The answer is right.

What could that mean? Rhino had no idea.

He fidgeted all through class that afternoon. Mrs. Imburgia called on him to read aloud, but he had lost his place.

"Sorry," Rhino said. "I had something on my mind."

"Try to keep your mind on your work, Ryan," his teacher said. She smiled and showed him where to read.

Rhino ran into Bella after school. "Big game tomorrow," she said. "Opening day!"

Rhino just nodded.

"The weather is supposed to be beautiful," Bella said. "I can't wait."

Rhino wasn't listening. He was looking around for Kerry. Finally, he saw her bright yellow shirt.

Kerry handed Rhino a sheet of paper. "My writing's in pencil," she said. "The black pen is Dylan's."

Rhino frowned as he looked at the note.

Knock-knock.
WHO'S THERE?
Hatch.
HATCH WHO?
Made you sneeze!

Neither writing looked like the notes he'd received earlier. Did Dylan know what they were trying to do? Maybe he'd disguised his writing this time.

Doubt it.

"No luck?" Bella asked.

Rhino shook his head.

"Forget about it then," Bella said. "We have plenty of bats. You can hit home runs with any of them."

Rhino knew that was true. But he wanted *his* bat. It all came down to one thing. The thing Grandpa James had talked about: *responsibility.*

I want Grandpa to think I'm responsible and be proud of me, Rhino thought. *And I want to be proud of myself. Hitting home runs makes me proud, but I want to be proud off the field and in school, too.*

Rhino walked away without saying good-bye to Kerry or Bella. He was carrying his science book and his math book. He had some catching up to do in those subjects. He'd been too distracted in class today.

It's just a bat, Rhino's thinker said. *Don't let it spoil anything else.*

· CHAPTER 5 ·
Cleanup Hitter

Saturday morning was bright and cool. Rhino woke up, threw on his uniform, and headed outside. Game day! He noticed that Grandpa had done more work in the backyard. There were a few fence posts several feet apart, and a patch of grass was missing. The project took up a lot of the yard.

Maybe Grandpa thinks I don't need to practice out here anymore, since I'm on a team, Rhino thought. *But I love coming out here and hanging out with Grandpa.* Still, Rhino knew that Grandpa enjoyed gardening. He'd spoken about making more room for tomatoes.

Cooper's voice broke into Rhino's thoughts.

"Let's go!" he called from the driveway. Rhino could tell Cooper was wearing his blue-and-white Mustangs uniform under a black wind jacket.

Cooper and Rhino hurried to the field to watch the first game, sitting on the top row of the bleachers. They'd been practicing here for weeks, but the place seemed different today. Lots of parents and brothers and sisters in the stands. Umpires in dark blue outfits. And the grass on the diamond had been newly mowed, leaving a sweet, fresh smell.

"We'll be out there soon," Cooper said.

Rhino rubbed his hands together. "Can't wait. I've been waiting for this for weeks!" He was too excited to sit still for long. After the first inning, he and Cooper went into the dugout.

When Dylan arrived, Rhino called to him. "Dylan!" he called sharply. "Get over here!"

Dylan trotted over. "What's up?" he said.

"Somebody took my bat the other day," Rhino said. He knew Dylan was aware of that, but he wanted to see his reaction.

"I heard," Dylan said. He stood a bit taller and glared down at Rhino. "What do you want me to do about it?"

"Give it back."

Dylan shook his head. "Why would I take it?" he asked. "I couldn't use it, could I? If I brought it to a game or a practice, everyone would know I stole it. Coach would boot me off the team."

Rhino scowled. "You could have taken it just to be mean."

Dylan crossed his arms. "I didn't take it," he said. "I'm no thief, Rhino. Get over it." And then he walked out of the dugout.

Rhino turned to Cooper. "What do you think?"

Cooper shrugged. "He seemed convincing."

Rhino looked at Cooper. "We'll see," he said. "You never know with Dylan." He glanced across the field and noticed that Coach Ray was watching. Had he seen the argument?

Soon Coach called the team to a spot behind the bleachers. He asked if anyone had taken Rhino's bat by mistake, but no one had.

Bella nudged Rhino. "How's it going?" she asked.

Rhino just grunted. He wanted to focus on getting ready to play.

The teams from the first game made their way off the field. "Everyone run around the bases a couple of times, then meet me at the bench," Coach said.

Rhino led the way around the bases, then ran to the dugout. Coach was holding up a sheet of paper. "This is the starting lineup for your first real game with the Mustangs."

1) Cooper	SS		6) Sara	3B
2) Bella	RF		7) Paul	CF
3) Dylan	P		8) Manny	2B
4) Rhino	1B		9) Gabe	C
5) Carlos	LF			

Rhino was glad to see that he'd be batting in the fourth spot. Coach called it "cleanup" because if any of the first three batters got on base, it was up to the fourth batter to get a hit so that the runners could score. You would clean up the bases. The best power hitters always went there.

"This is what we've been practicing for. So go out there and have fun. Do your best. Enjoy it!" said Coach.

I will, thought Rhino. *I just wish I knew where my bat was.* And then the game began.

Rhino struck out to end the bottom of the first inning. The Bears had a hard-throwing pitcher with a tricky sinker.

I'll figure him out, Rhino thought. *Next at bat: wham!*

Rhino made a few routine plays at first base, catching a pop fly and taking throws from second base and shortstop after ground balls. The Bears managed one run in the second inning.

In the third inning, Rhino walked over to the pile of bats leaning against the fence. He picked up one bat to test its weight. *Too heavy,* he thought. Rhino looked at the different lengths. One with a blue stripe around the handle was longer than the rest. He picked that one up and swung it a couple of times. None of these felt as good as his own. He chose one that was a little heavier than he'd used the first time up.

Things were looking good. Cooper was on second base after hitting a single, and Dylan was on first. There were two outs. Rhino was ready to clear the bases and put the Mustangs into the lead with one swing.

"Bring them home!" came a call from the dugout.

"Smack that ball!" came another.

Rhino gripped the bat and squinted toward the pitcher. *Contact,* he thought. *Make contact and send that ball over the fence.*

The first pitch was outside, and Rhino didn't even flinch.

"Good eye!" yelled Cooper. He took a few steps away from second base.

The next pitch was a little high, but it was straight down the middle. Rhino focused on the ball and swung hard. The ball took off like a rocket, deep into right-center field.

"That's gone!" someone yelled as Rhino raced toward first base.

Clank! The ball bounced off the fence and back onto the field. Rhino kept sprinting, rounding first and striding for second. He slid in safely and looked up. Had he driven in both runners?

Dylan dove back to third as the throw came in. So only Cooper had scored. Still, Rhino's double had tied the game.

"Come on, Carlos!" Rhino called as the next batter stepped up. He and Dylan could both score on a single.

But Carlos struck out.

Coach announced some substitutions as they headed into the fourth inning. "I'm going to switch some of you around so everyone gets a chance to play," Coach said. "You know these games are only six innings long." He pointed at Carlos. "Take a breather and nice job."

Carlos nodded and took a seat on the bench. His Mustangs jersey was too big for him. His shoulders and neck were tiny compared to the giant collar and armholes of the shirt.

"Serves you right," Dylan muttered to Carlos. "You struck out twice."

Carlos looked away. Rhino had heard that English was not Carlos's native language, but he'd never heard Carlos say anything.

Rhino grabbed Dylan's arm. "Watch your mouth," he said. "We're all teammates."

Dylan pulled his arm free and headed for the pitcher's mound.

"Good effort," Rhino said to Carlos. Rhino was beginning to think of himself as the team leader. He wouldn't stand for any bullying.

Carlos gave Rhino a small smile and sat up straighter.

The Bears scored twice in the fourth, but the Mustangs tied it up. Rhino made good contact again, smacking a sizzling line drive that landed squarely in the second baseman's glove for an out.

The teams were tied 3–3 as they headed into the sixth inning. Rhino punched his glove and bounced on his toes. The Mustangs would have the top of the batting order up next inning. If they could hold the Bears scoreless, they'd have a great chance to win in their last licks.

Dylan walked the first batter, then struck out the next.

"No batter!" the infielders yelled. "Whizz it past her, Dylan."

Dylan threw a fastball. The batter connected,

knocking it over Manny's head at second base and deep into the outfield.

Rhino turned to Bella and waited for the throw. The ball came to him on a bounce, and he spun toward home plate. The runner was rounding third, and Rhino fired the ball to the catcher. Both runners scrambled back to the bases.

The game was still tied, but the Bears had runners on second and third with only one out.

Coach Ray called time-out and walked to the pitcher's mound. The catcher walked out, too.

Rhino blew out his breath. "Let's hold 'em," he hollered.

Dylan rose to the occasion. He struck out the next batter on three pitches.

"Two outs!" Rhino called, holding up two fingers. "Play to first!" One more out would end the inning. There was no reason to throw home.

Rhino took an extra step back. The Bears' cleanup hitter was at bat, and he'd already hit a pair of doubles today.

Dylan wound up. Here came the pitch.

Plunk. To everyone's surprise, the batter bunted! The ball rolled up the first baseline. Rhino charged toward it.

Dylan got to the ball first. He scooped it up, pivoted toward first, and stopped short.

No one was covering the base.

The runner from third crossed home plate.

Rhino gulped. He stared at Dylan.

"What are you doing?" Dylan asked sharply.

"I was chasing the ball." Rhino felt the wind go out of him. He'd made a critical mistake. The Bears were ahead, and it was Rhino's fault.

"That's okay," Coach said, clapping his hands. "Good hustle, Rhino."

Rhino shook his head and walked back to his position.

Dylan struck out the next batter to end the rally. Rhino tossed his glove onto the bench. He was fuming.

I'll make up for that mistake as soon as I get to bat.

· CHAPTER 6 ·
No Excuses

Rhino felt a surge of energy as Cooper led off the bottom of the sixth with another single. It was his second hit of the game.

Unless there was a double play, Rhino was certain to bat. He cheered for Bella, but she popped up to second base for the first out.

Dylan stepped in. He'd hit a pair of singles so far.

It was a long at bat. Dylan hit several foul balls before running the count to three balls, two strikes.

"A walk's as good as a hit," called Bella.

Dylan lined another shot out of bounds.

"Straighten it out," Rhino said.

But Dylan went down swinging. Two outs.

Dylan stared straight ahead as he walked back to the dugout. He didn't make eye contact with Rhino, but muttered, "It's up to you."

I'm more than ready, Rhino thought.

Rhino looked at the scoreboard: Bears 4, Mustangs 3. Last inning, last chance.

He nodded to Cooper at first base. Placed the bat on his shoulder.

The Bears' coach called time. Rhino kicked gently at the dirt and waited as the coach spoke to the pitcher. The coach ran back to his dugout.

Rhino took a deep breath. The pitcher wound up into his motion.

Whack! Rhino connected solidly and the ball soared toward deep center field. Everyone in the bleachers stood to watch. The Mustangs players erupted with cheers.

Rhino rounded first. He heard another huge cheer.

The Bears' shortstop leaped with his fist in the air. The second baseman let out a *whoop.*

Rhino glanced to the outfield. The center fielder was holding up his glove. The ball was tucked inside.

Rhino stopped running and stared at the outfielder. The Bears were shouting and jumping.

Game over.

If I had my bat, that would have been gone, Rhino told himself. *Six more inches and it would have been a homer.*

Rhino walked slowly to the dugout. *No excuses,* he told himself. Still, he couldn't help thinking that his own bat would have made the difference. A loss in their first game.

Rhino felt a tug on his sleeve. He turned to see Carlos looking up at him. "Nice hit," Carlos said in a shy voice. He held up his palm and Rhino gave him a high five. But Rhino felt awful.

Coach congratulated them on a tough, well-played game. But how could Rhino be the team leader after a game like that? He'd made a big mistake on defense and a near-miss in his final at bat.

Bella smiled at him. Rhino looked away.

"Here," Bella said, holding out a fresh water bottle. "Take a drink."

"No, thanks," Rhino said. He followed Cooper out of the dugout and didn't look back. Bella looked down at the ground and kicked a rock across the infield dirt.

"There's another game in a few minutes," Cooper said. "Want to watch?"

Rhino shrugged. "I guess," he said. Then he realized that he'd left his sweatshirt in the dugout. He ran back for it and met Cooper over in the bleachers.

Rhino was frustrated. He didn't say much through the start of the game.

"Thirsty?" Cooper asked after two innings.

Rhino nodded. "Let's get a soda."

He reached into his sweatshirt pocket for some money. He pulled out a folded sheet of paper. It was another note.

Rhino read it out loud. "Clue three: Pay more attention and your bat will come back."

Pay attention to *what*? Rhino had no idea. He always tried to stay focused. "Any idea who wrote this?" he asked Cooper.

"Somebody on the team, I guess," Cooper said.

Rhino nodded. "Somebody like our pitcher, I think." His thinker told him not to accuse Dylan again without evidence. But this time, Rhino thought his thinker was wrong.

"I've got some homework I need to finish," Rhino told Cooper. "I should get home." Cooper and Rhino slapped palms and pointed at each other. It was their handshake. Rhino started walking home.

Later that afternoon, Rhino sat with Grandpa James on the porch and told him about the game.

"Sounds as if you played well," Grandpa said. "Sorry I missed it." C.J.'s game had been at the same time. "I can only be one place at a time," Grandpa said with a grin. "I'll be at your next one."

Rhino told himself that he'd play better when Grandpa came to see him.

"You hit the ball hard," Grandpa said. "No one gets a hit every time. And for your first game at a new position, you did great."

"Except for that one play," Rhino said.

"That was a tough one," Grandpa replied. "But remember that even the Major Leaguers make errors. It's part of the game, and you will continue to learn from your mistakes."

Rhino nodded. He felt better. "Next time," he said.

"You've got a whole season," Grandpa said. "You'll have plenty of chances. Keep working hard, keep learning, keep your spirits up. And have fun."

"I will." Today's game *had* been fun. It was tough to lose, but they'd have another game in a few days.

Think positive, Rhino's thinker said. *Leaders take the good with the bad.*

Something else was nagging at Rhino, though. "You've been working hard in the backyard," he said. "Expanding the garden, huh?"

Grandpa smiled. "I want to see more growth."

"It looks like there won't be much room to bat."

"We'll see," Grandpa said. "We'll see."

Rhino nodded, but he felt sad. Did Grandpa think Rhino was too old for playing in the yard? Rhino loved being on a baseball team, but he enjoyed those hours in the yard with Grandpa just as much. Maybe more.

He wasn't ready to give that up.

· CHAPTER 7 ·
Raising the Stakes

Over the weekend, Rhino and C.J. went to the park to throw around the football. It was a lot of fun having his brother to himself for a while. C.J. could throw bombs, and Rhino would have to dive to try and catch them. But the entire time Rhino was distracted, thinking about those clues. *Pay attention? The answer is right?* He couldn't figure it out.

After he found another note in his school desk on Monday, he still had no idea what the clues meant.

Getting your bat back is up to you.

That sounded familiar. He thought and thought, and finally he remembered. Dylan had said, "It's up to you" when Rhino went to bat in the last inning of Saturday's game.

Maybe someone else was writing the notes for Dylan so his writing wouldn't be recognized.

This has gone on long enough, Rhino decided. *My bat isn't lost. Someone has it. And that isn't fair.* Rhino's patience was running out.

He decided to take this up with Dylan as soon as he saw him. That would make Rhino feel better.

He tried to put it out of his mind until then and concentrate on his classwork.

Midway through the morning, Rhino saw Dylan walk by the classroom. Rhino put up his hand and asked for permission to get a drink.

"Ryan, it's nearly lunchtime," Mrs. Imburgia said.

"I'm *very* thirsty," Rhino said.

"All right," the teacher replied.

The hallway was empty except for Dylan. Rhino called to him.

Dylan stopped and turned. Rhino read the words SURF'S UP on his T-shirt.

"Hey, Mustang," Dylan said.

Rhino walked over and kept his voice at a whisper. He showed Dylan the new note. "Do you know anything about this?" he asked.

"I already told you I'm not involved."

"Listen," Rhino said. "You want to win, right? Well, I'll hit better with my own bat."

Dylan shrugged. "The bat doesn't matter so much. A lot of them are alike."

"That's not the point." Rhino stepped closer so he was just a few inches from Dylan. He leaned in and raised his voice. "It's *my* bat."

Dylan spoke louder, too. "And it's *your* problem. Not mine."

"You're the problem!" Rhino said.

Rhino turned when he heard his teacher's voice. "What are you boys doing?" Mrs. Imburgia said from the doorway.

"I was minding my own business," Dylan said. "Rhino started this."

"It's finished now," Mrs. Imburgia said. "And if I hear you two arguing like that again, you'll *both* go to the principal."

Dylan blushed and walked away.

Rhino swallowed hard. Grandpa James would not be happy if he got a phone call from the principal. That might be the end of baseball for a while.

Mrs. Imburgia's expression seemed to be half a

smile and half a frown. Rhino had never been in trouble in her classroom.

"That didn't seem like you, Ryan," she said.

"Dylan's on my baseball team," Rhino mumbled. "He can be a pain."

"We'll leave it at that this time," the teacher said. "But I don't want to see that kind of behavior again."

Rhino nodded. "Sorry," he said. "Thanks for not sending us to the principal's office. It won't happen again."

At least not in school, Rhino thought. *I'm not done with Dylan yet. I want my bat back.*

At lunch, Rhino sat with the dinosaur group, but his mind was on his bat. He chewed his PB&J sandwich, munched on his BBQ chips, and didn't speak for a long time.

Bella asked, "What's wrong?"

Rhino unfolded the new note and showed it to her. "How can it be 'up to me' if I don't even know where the bat is?"

Cooper reached over and picked up the paper. "I vote that we talk about this note instead of stegosaurs," he said. Cooper had been shy at the lunch table when they first started sitting there. Now he had no problem talking in front of his new friends.

"That's fine by me," said Kerry.

Rhino told everyone about the other three clues.

"Pay attention to what?" Kerry asked, reading from the note.

"I don't know," Rhino said. "These clues don't make sense. I've thought about them for days."

"This is getting us nowhere," Bella said. "The only question we should be thinking about right now is 'What did stegosaurs eat?'"

"We need to help Rhino," Cooper said.

"There's nothing we can do," Bella replied. She turned to Rhino. "Whoever has the bat will give it back," she said. "Maybe you did something wrong, and they're waiting for you to make it right."

"I didn't do anything wrong," Rhino said.

Bella raised one eyebrow at him. "Are you sure about that?" she asked. Then, turning to the group sitting at the table, she said, "Stegosaurs! I read that their brains weren't any bigger than a golf ball."

Others chimed in with more stegosaur facts. Rhino read the new clue again and stuck it in his pocket. There was no sense wasting a good lunchtime worrying about it. "I heard that they ate rocks," Rhino said.

"No way," said Kerry. "Why would they do that?"

"Someone was messing with you, Rhino," Cooper said with a laugh.

Rhino shook his head. He'd read it in three different books. "Birds do it, so why not dinosaurs?" he said. "Having rocks in their stomachs helped to grind up the food. You can look it up. I'm serious."

"Like a chicken's gizzard?" Cooper asked.

"Yeah," Rhino said. "Scientists think lots of plant-eaters did that."

"Pretty weird and gross," said Kerry. She glanced at the clock. "Almost out of time. Everyone find out more crazy dino facts for tomorrow."

"Bring a tasty lunch, everybody," Rhino said. "No rocks."

Bella got up and walked away from the table first. Rhino watched her walk away. *Could I have done something wrong and not know it?* Rhino thought. He grabbed his book bag and left the cafeteria with everyone else.

· CHAPTER 8 ·
Learning the Ropes

Rhino and Cooper ran all the way to the field after school on Tuesday. This would be their first practice session since Saturday's game.

"Slow down a little," Cooper said. "You don't want to tire yourself out."

"No chance!" Rhino said. "I can't wait to get there."

Coach Ray and Bella were already at the field. Bella waved to him, but Rhino just ran past her. *She didn't even want to help me solve the clues at lunch. All she wanted to do was talk about dinosaurs.* He scooped up a baseball and threw it to Cooper, then ran to catch the return throw. Cooper threw it high in the air toward second base.

"Throw it here!" Bella said.

Rhino glanced over, but he tossed the ball to Cooper instead. "Here comes Manny," he said to Bella. "Throw with him."

Coach soon clapped his hands and yelled for the players to gather in the dugout. Rhino saw Dylan scrambling over the right-field fence, late as usual. Dylan sprinted across the field.

"We've been doing some good work on the baseball field," Coach said. "But we have work to do *off* the field. Some of you still forget that this is a team."

Rhino shifted his feet. Coach wouldn't know about his argument with Dylan at school. But he did know about their quarrel before the last game.

Coach pointed to Cooper's feet. "No cleats today, Cooper?" he asked.

"I forgot," Cooper said.

Coach pointed to Manny. "What about your cap?" he asked.

"I left it at home," Manny said. "Sorry about that."

Coach nodded. "As I've said before, show up ready to play. That means full equipment." He turned to Dylan. "And just as important, show up *on time*. As athletes, we need to take responsibility."

There was that word again. *Responsibility.* Rhino's thinker had done a lot of work on that. But was he living up to it?

"More important than any of this is teamwork and sportsmanship," Coach said. "Each of us needs to treat the others the way we'd expect to be treated. If I see players arguing again, their playing time will be cut."

Rhino gulped. He knew Coach was referring to him. His stomach felt squirmy.

"Even if they're the best players on the team," Coach added.

Rhino glanced at Dylan, then looked down. Coach probably noticed that Dylan had been mean to Carlos, too. Rhino wished Coach had seen him stand up for his teammate.

Coach smiled. "Most of you are new at this, so I know you'll make mistakes," he said. "Now, let's get on the field and prepare for the next game. I watched the Falcons play on Saturday, and they're very good."

Rhino walked quickly to first base. He wondered if he should apologize to Dylan. After all, Rhino had started both arguments. Then again, maybe Dylan had started it all by taking the bat.

I'll wait and see, Rhino thought. *If it turns out Dylan is innocent, I'll definitely apologize.*

Cooper was pitching today, and Dylan moved to shortstop. Bella trotted past Rhino on her way to right field. She winked at him.

Rhino smiled. Bella was always nice to him, and he knew he'd been ignoring her lately. *Treat everyone the way you want to be treated.* "Play great, Bella," he said.

"You too."

Rhino swung his arms to loosen up some more. *Now, focus on baseball and have some fun,* he thought.

"Let's get ready for a win on Thursday!" Rhino called.

Rhino stayed at first base for most of the practice session even though Coach shifted some of the other players around. Dylan moved over to pitcher and Cooper slid to shortstop. Coach gave Rhino more tips. The most important was to get a feel for where to stand in every situation. Rhino had to be able to field any ball hit close to his right or left. He also needed to be near enough to the base to get there in time for throws from the other infielders.

Rhino knew that it was a very important position, and he liked the feeling of being involved in almost every play. *I'm in charge of this infield!*

"The more experience you get, the more comfortable you'll be," Coach said. "First base takes a lot of learning."

Toward the end of practice, Cooper hit a high pop fly between first and second base. Rhino judged it, shouted, "Me, me, me!" and moved into position to catch it.

"Smart call," Coach said. He'd been telling the players all season to call for the ball to warn the others so there wouldn't be a collision. They were starting to get it, but some of them forgot. Rhino always got that right. Grandpa James had taught him to do that.

"Last batter!" Coach called.

Rhino knew that was him. He tossed the ball to Dylan on the mound.

Rhino ran to the dugout. He picked up a couple of bats and looked them over. Then he saw a familiar bat in the rack.

It was his!

· CHAPTER 9 ·
The Right Reply

Rhino didn't care how the bat got there. He was so happy he could burst.

He walked to the batter's box with a big grin and tapped the bat on home plate. *Give me your best pitch,* he thought. *It'll be "bye-bye baseball."*

Dylan looked intense. He went into his wind-up and fired the ball. Rhino followed it, timing his swing. With all his might, he took a powerful cut.

Whoosh. The ball popped into the catcher's glove. Dylan pumped his fist.

Rhino let out a deep breath and looked toward

the center field fence. *One strike,* he thought. *No big deal.*

"Don't overswing," Coach called. "Meet the ball."

Rhino had heard that often from Grandpa James. He had plenty of power. He just needed to make contact.

He lined the next pitch over Manny's head. It dropped safely into right field, and Bella fielded it.

"Take a few more swings," Coach said.

Rhino hit one deep into center field, then banged one off the fence in left. His bat felt perfect.

Watch out, Falcons, he thought. *Thursday night will belong to the Mustangs.*

Bella pulled Rhino aside after practice. "Great hitting," she said.

"Thanks. My bat makes a difference."

"Did you figure out who took it?"

Rhino shook his head. "I guess it doesn't matter," he said. "What matters is that I got it back."

"That's the *right* answer," Bella said.

Rhino gave her a puzzled look.

"Right," she said. "As in right fielder."

"*You* took it?" Rhino was shocked. Bella was always so nice to him.

Bella shrugged. "I just meant it as a practical joke," she said. "I was going to give it right back, but then you started ignoring me."

"No, I didn't," Rhino said. "I was just distracted. *Because* of the bat."

"I'm really sorry," Bella said. "I hope you'll forgive me. I want us to be friends."

"Where did you hide it?"

"After that practice, I put it under our car seat so my dad wouldn't find it," Bella said. "I told him all about it before practice today. He said I can't watch TV or play video games for a week."

"Why didn't you tell me before practice?" Rhino asked.

"My dad wanted you to concentrate on playing first base today. That's why he had you bat last. So you'd find the bat on your own."

Rhino laughed. "That was a *bad* practical joke," he said. "Not cool!"

"I'm sorry," Bella replied.

Rhino knew that he also had someone to say sorry to.

This wouldn't be easy, but Rhino stood proudly. It was all about responsibility and honesty. He'd been wrong to accuse anyone unless he'd been certain. *Dylan knows how to be a big-mouthed bully, but he was right about one thing. He's not a thief.*

"Hey, Dylan!" Rhino called. He walked toward his teammate.

Dylan squinted and puffed out his chest. He waited for Rhino to speak.

"I found my bat," Rhino said.

"So I see."

"I was wrong to say you took it," Rhino continued. "I'm sorry."

Dylan nodded slowly. Rhino stuck out his hand. After a few seconds, Dylan shook it.

"I guess you had some good reasons to assume I took your bat," Dylan said. "I gave you a hard time early in the season, and I shouldn't have done that."

"Right," Rhino replied. He grinned a little. "You sure did."

"Apology accepted," Dylan said. He shrugged. "Let's get past it and win some games."

"One more thing," Rhino said, thinking about Carlos. "We need to treat every player with respect, not just the ones who get all the hits. You know what I mean?"

Dylan nodded. "Fair enough," he said. "I know exactly what you mean."

Grandpa and C.J. had picked up a pizza for dinner. Rhino filled them in about the bat.

"Kids do strange things," Grandpa said. "Sounds like you're ready to forgive. That's a good thing."

Rhino did feel proud that he'd accepted Bella's apology and given one to Dylan.

"How did he react?" C.J. asked. "You and he have been battling for weeks."

"He actually understood where I was coming from," Rhino said. "I think we can finally start to get along now." He grinned. "Until he pulls something else. Knowing Dylan, he probably will."

Rhino took a giant bite of his cheesy pizza. Grandpa and C.J. would be at Thursday's game. Rhino couldn't wait. Now he could finally concentrate on baseball.

"We need a win," he said. He still felt a little bad about the way they'd lost on Saturday. That mistake on the bunt. The long fly out to end the game.

Pressure. It could be a good thing or a bad thing. Rhino felt pressure to help his team to a victory. But that pressure was coming from himself.

Rhino knew he was becoming a leader on his

team. But so far, they'd only lost. Thursday was the next big test. For the Mustangs and for Rhino.

Grandpa stood and put one hand each on Rhino's and C.J.'s shoulders. "I have something to show you both," he said. "I took the day off from work and finished the backyard project today."

"It'll be like a farm back there," C.J. said with a laugh. "How many tomato plants will fit?"

Rhino tried to laugh, too, but he was sad about losing part of the yard.

But there were no plants in the new space. Grandpa had enclosed the area with black-mesh netting. A white panel of wood the shape of home plate was embedded in the ground near one end of the enclosure.

"A batting cage?" C.J. said. "You built us a batting cage, Grandpa?"

Grandpa laughed. "I got tired of chasing every ball Rhino hit out into the street. Plus, it was only a matter of time before he started breaking windows.

With this net, the ball will stay in the cage, no matter how hard he hits it."

Rhino's mouth hung open in surprise. He ran to the cage.

"This will be great for you, too, C.J.," Grandpa said. "You haven't been able to practice batting back here since you were smaller than Rhino. With both of you enjoying baseball, I figured it was time to expand your opportunities."

"Will you still pitch to me?" Rhino asked.

"Of course," Grandpa said. "In fact, let's try it right now. Go get the new bat, Little Rhino. We'll see if I can still strike you out!"

· CHAPTER 10 ·
Pulling for a Win

Grandpa made an early dinner on Thursday of pork chops and mashed potatoes, and Rhino did all his homework as soon as he got home from school. He threw on his baseball uniform and dusted off his cleats.

He wanted everything to be perfect.

"Hurry up, C.J.," Rhino called up the stairs.

C.J. came running down. He was wearing his cap from the middle-school team and a T-shirt that said FALCONS FOOTBALL.

"Wrong team!" Rhino said with a laugh. "We're playing against the Falcons."

"Not these Falcons," C.J. said. But he ran back up to change.

"That's better," Rhino said when C.J. returned in a solid green shirt. "We don't need to give them any extra help!"

Half the team was already at the field when Rhino showed up. He took a throw from Manny and fired the ball to Dylan. *Glad to see Dylan got here on time for once,* Rhino thought. He could smell popcorn and french fries cooking at the refreshment stand, and music was playing from the announcer's booth.

Great atmosphere. Big-time! Rhino thought.

Coach had changed the lineup a little, but Rhino would still be batting cleanup. Cooper was still leading off.

1) Cooper	SS		6) Paul	CF
2) Gabe	C		7) Manny	2B
3) Dylan	P		8) Sara	3B
4) Rhino	1B		9) Carlos	LF
5) Bella	RF			

The Mustangs were the visitors today, so they batted first. Rhino swung his arms until he felt loose. He picked up his bat and gripped it.

But Cooper, Gabe, and Dylan all went down quickly. Rhino was left in the on-deck circle as the inning ended.

"Let's give them the same treatment!" he called. He threw a quick grounder to Sara at third base, who fielded it and threw to Manny at second. Manny threw it to Cooper at shortstop, and Cooper made the long throw back to first. Coach called throwing the ball like this going "around the horn." Rhino loved to do it at the start of every inning. *I control this infield,* he thought. *I set the tone.*

He could tell that his teammates were in high spirits tonight. They yelled when Dylan struck out the first batter, and they cheered when Manny made a routine play on the next one, tossing the ball to Rhino. They raced off the field when Gabe caught a pop-up behind the plate to end the frame.

"Right over the fence, Rhino!" Bella called as he picked up his bat.

"Hit a dinger!" Cooper yelled.

Rhino felt a surge of energy. He remembered Coach's words from practice though. *Don't overswing. Meet the ball.*

He'd studied the Falcons' pitcher in the first inning. His first pitch to all three batters had been an inside fastball. Then a curve. Then another fastball. Rhino could hit any of those pitches but knowing the pattern might help.

Just as he expected, the first pitch was a fastball, low and inside. Rhino let it go by and the umpire called a ball.

"Good eye!" Coach called.

"Wait for your pitch," said Bella.

The second pitch was a tricky curve, and it caught the outside corner to even the count at a ball and a strike. Rhino stepped back and wiped his hand on his jersey.

Fastball, he thought.

He was right. He blasted the ball deep into right-center. Rhino tore up the first baseline and kept going, streaking toward second. He slid into the base and popped right up, beating the throw by ten feet.

Rhino could hear C.J.'s and Grandpa's voices among the cheers from the crowd. The pitcher scowled and dug his toe into the mound.

Rhino wiped some reddish dirt from the knee of his pants. *Looks good,* he thought. *Looks like a hit.*

"Bring him home, Bella!" yelled Cooper.

But Bella struck out. So did Paul and Manny.

Rhino didn't get farther than second base.

"Okay!" he called. "Heads up. We'll get in a batting groove next inning!"

But just like last time, the Mustangs fell behind. The Falcons scored a pair of runs when their pitcher lined a double with two runners on base.

"Let's get 'em back," Rhino said between innings. But Rhino struck out. He didn't bat again until the fifth.

Better eye this time, he told himself. Gabe was on first base with one out. The Mustangs needed some runs.

Rhino was still thinking about the strikeout in his last at bat. *Shake it off,* his thinker said.

He let a high pitch go past for a ball. Rhino took the bat off his shoulder. He took a couple of practice swings. *This bat feels perfect in my hands.* The next pitch was about to come his way. He dug his foot into the dirt. Pulled back the bat.

Crack! That one felt solid! The ball rose quickly, soaring over the second baseman, over the right fielder, over the fence, and deep into the parking lot.

"Home run!" yelled Cooper. The Mustangs roared.

Rhino didn't go into a "home run trot." He was too excited. He sprinted around the bases and came down hard on home plate. Gabe met him at the plate and grabbed him in a bear hug. The other teammates lined up for high fives.

The game was tied, 2–2.

"This one's ours," Rhino said as he entered the dugout. "We're rolling now!"

But the Falcons answered in the bottom of the fifth. The first batter drew a walk, and the next drove him in with a triple.

Dylan looked rattled.

"No problem!" Rhino called. "Throw some strikes."

But Dylan couldn't seem to find the plate. He threw four straight balls, and the Falcons had another base runner. Two on, no outs, and one run already in.

Coach called time-out and walked toward the pitcher's mound.

One thing was clear. The Mustangs were in trouble.

· CHAPTER 11 ·
Butterflies

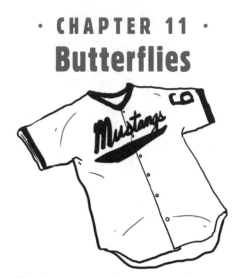

Rhino walked over to the mound, too. Gabe came up from behind the plate. Coach said it was time to change pitchers.

"Good work, Dylan," Rhino said. "We'll get that run back and more."

Dylan just grunted and looked down.

"Your arm's tired," Coach said. "Switch positions with Cooper."

Cooper took the ball and stepped onto the mound. Coach, Dylan, and Gabe went back to their places. Rhino hesitated for a moment. "Pick this guy off," he whispered. He remembered that the kid who'd just walked had stolen second base earlier in the game.

Cooper glanced at Rhino.

"He's itching to run," Rhino said softly. "He'll never expect a pick-off move before you even throw a pitch."

Rhino trotted back to first base, and Cooper tossed a few warm-up pitches.

The umpire signaled for play to resume. Rhino stood a few feet from the base. The runner took three steps away and leaned toward second. Rhino was certain that he would try to steal.

Cooper played it perfectly. He stared toward home plate and went into his wind-up. As the base runner took one more step, Cooper pivoted and fired the ball to first. Rhino sprinted over. The runner stumbled, then dove back. Rhino tagged him just in time. The umpire yelled, "Out!"

"Beautiful!" Coach called. The Mustangs in the dugout hollered and shook the fence.

Rhino tried not to grin. He'd made a smart

call. He threw the ball to Cooper and got back into position. The Falcons were a run ahead, and that runner on third could give them a bigger edge.

"One out!" Rhino called, holding up his index finger.

Cooper took a lot of the pressure off by getting a strikeout. Two outs. The next batter hit a long fly ball to left field. Rhino held his breath as the ball soared toward the fence.

Carlos ran toward it, reaching out his glove. He made the catch, then leaped with joy. Three outs! The base runner was stranded.

Dylan, Cooper, and Rhino waited in the infield as Carlos sprinted toward the dugout. They slapped him on the back and hooted.

The Mustangs entered the sixth inning trailing, 3–2.

Let's change that in a hurry, Rhino thought.

The first batter lined a pitch toward second base, but the shortstop made a great catch.

So close, Rhino thought. The Mustangs needed two base runners or he wouldn't get to bat.

Cooper walked, and he moved to second on Gabe's groundout.

Rhino caught Dylan's eye. They nodded at each other. "Here's your chance to make up for that rough inning," Rhino said. "Bring Cooper home."

Dylan watched two pitches go by, one for a ball and one for a strike. He drove the third pitch right up the middle.

Cooper rounded third, but the throw from center field was right on target. Cooper scrambled back, but Dylan managed to reach second.

It was set up perfectly for Rhino. *Here comes my second home run of the game!*

Rhino thought back to the last game. That long fly out had ended it.

"Here we go!" shouted C.J., who was sitting in the bleachers behind first base. "Two more ribbies, Rhino!"

Rhino knew that "ribbies" meant RBIs: runs batted in. Two would give the Mustangs the lead. But a home run would drive in three. It made him happy to know C.J. believed in him.

Find your pitch, Rhino thought. *Any safe hit will bring in those runs.*

This pitch looked perfect.

Rhino swung hard and felt the solid connection between the ball and the bat. He raced up the first baseline. The ball was high and deep into right field.

But at the last second it drifted foul.

"Straighten it out," Bella called from the on-deck circle.

Rhino tapped his cleats with the bat. He waited for the next pitch.

Another smooth swing. Another solid connection. The ball bounced behind second base and rolled quickly into the outfield. Cooper scored. Dylan, too. Rhino rounded first base and pumped his fist. The Mustangs had the lead!

Bella grounded out to end the rally, but Rhino was excited. "Great defense, now!" he called. "One-two-three and this game is over."

They tossed the ball around the horn and made a lot of chatter. Cooper had only thrown a few pitches so his arm was ready.

The first batter hit a fast ground ball to Dylan, and he made an accurate throw to first.

"One away!" Rhino yelled, holding up a finger.

Rhino fielded the next grounder himself. He had plenty of time to get to the base, so he waved Cooper off and ran to the bag.

"Two down!" he called.

Now Rhino felt the butterflies again. They were one out away from a win, but anything could happen.

"It ain't over till it's over," C.J. called from the stands, quoting the Hall of Fame catcher Yogi Berra.

And as if to prove that, the Falcons' next batter smashed a long fly ball that flew just outside the foul pole in right field.

"Strike one!" called the umpire, but it easily could have been a homer.

Rhino had held his breath as he watched the long foul ball. He blew it out and shook his wrists.

Cooper's fastball went by for strike two. Rhino felt another surge of excitement. He concentrated on the batter, ready to react.

Crack! The ball seemed to sizzle as it bounced hard to Rhino's right. He darted toward it and knocked it down with his glove as he fell to his knees.

Cooper and the batter were racing toward first base. Rhino scooped up the ball with his bare hand and flung it toward Cooper. Cooper grabbed it, leaped to the base, and twisted to avoid a collision.

"Out!" yelled the umpire.

Game over!

Rhino ran to Cooper. They jumped and slapped their palms together and pointed at each other. The rest of the Mustangs ran over, too.

Nothing could feel better than this!

"Great hitting and great fielding," Grandpa James said as he gave Rhino a hug.

"Great teammates, too," Rhino said. "We can win the championship, I know it." *One day we can win the World Series.*

"You've got a long season ahead," Grandpa replied. "But you did look like champs today."

Rhino was glad he only had to wait two days for the next game. Saturday couldn't get here soon enough. But he didn't want to forget today just yet. Three hits. Some smart plays in the field.

And a giant win for the Mustangs.

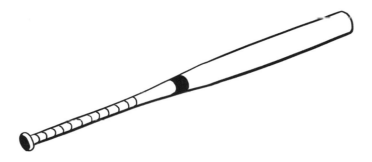

A HERO AT ANY POSITION!

HERE'S A SNEAK PEEK AT BOOK #3!

he pitcher looked worried. Little Rhino was sort of nervous, too, but he was ready. Butterflies were part of baseball! He blew out his breath and stepped into the batter's box.

Rhino felt sweat trickling down his neck. The air was warm and still. *This pitcher knows I can hit,* he thought. *It's me against him.*

The game was tied. Rhino's teammate Cooper had reached second base, and he would score if Rhino got another hit. With two outs, the game was riding on Rhino.

"Bring him home!" came a shout from the Mustangs' dugout.

"Strike him out!" came a call from the other side of the field.

Rhino watched the first pitch go by. It was way outside. He stepped back and wiped some dirt from the knee of his baseball pants. That was from sliding into third a couple of innings ago with a triple.

This pitch, he thought. *This is the one!*

The pitcher threw a fastball. It was low but straight down the middle. Rhino pulled back his bat and swung hard.

He felt a pop, but it wasn't his bat hitting the ball. A sharp pain surged through Rhino's ankle. He fell to the dirt and winced.

"Yow!" Rhino yelled. The umpire called time out and Coach Ray ran from the dugout.

Rhino tried to get up, but his coach told him to stay still. He gently grabbed Rhino's right ankle. "Here?" he asked.

Rhino nodded. He blinked his eyes and bit down on his lip. It hurt, but Rhino tried to fight off the pain. "I'll be okay," Rhino said. He reached for his bat.

"I think that you're done for today," Coach Ray said.

"I'm all right," Rhino replied. He flexed the ankle to show his coach that it was okay. "See?" But it did hurt.

"That's a good sign that you can move it, but it

will probably start to swell," Coach said. "Let's get some ice on it."

Coach and the umpire helped Rhino to the dugout. They wrapped an ice pack on the ankle and propped Rhino's foot up on a couple of sweatshirts.

"Tough break," said Rhino's teammate Bella. She shook her dark ponytail and looked concerned. Bella was Coach Ray's daughter, and she had become a good friend to Rhino.

"It better *not* be a break," Rhino said. He didn't see what the big deal was. He thought he could have continued batting.

I get little bumps and bruises all the time, Rhino thought. *They never slow me down.*